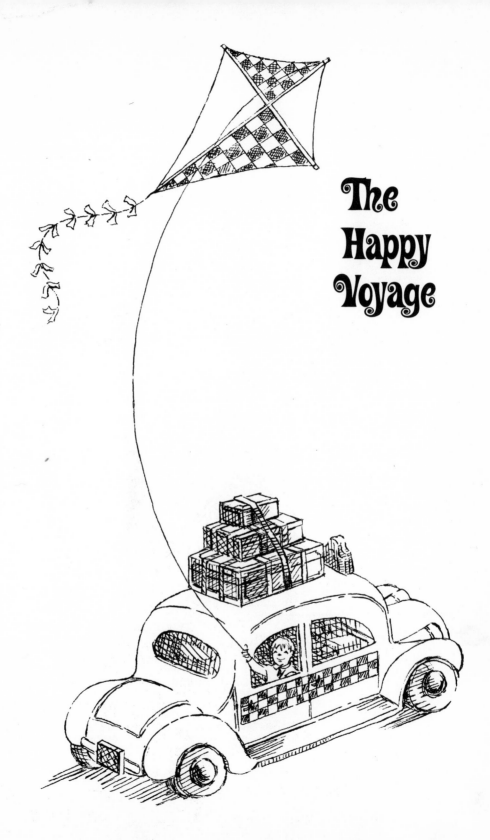

The Happy Voyage

The Happy Voyage

Story and Pictures by

JUDITH GWYN BROWN

THE MACMILLAN COMPANY, NEW YORK
COLLIER-MACMILLAN LIMITED, LONDON

For my mother

The water was bright, the sun was yellow.
Three smokestacks boomed a frightening bellow.
And Daniel MacPherson Robert Dufore,
Who had never traveled alone before,
Was sailing to England for a three-month vacation
To visit his aunt—his father's relation.

Dan's mother and father gave him the key
To unlock cabin number two-twenty-three.
It was very neat but awfully small,
With a chair and a bed fastened to the wall.
Standing next to the polished door,
Dan saw heaped on the shining floor
Trunks and gifts, an umbrella for rain,
And a basket of fruit wrapped in pink cellophane.

Dan's mother said, "This cabin is nice,"
And then she gave him some good advice.

"Don't take cold, do eat your greens;
Our best to all at Aunt Justine's;
Be sure you use a brush and a comb,
And write to us every day at home."
Then she kissed him and said with a tear,
"We must go now. Have a good time, dear."
And just for a moment Dan's heart sank
As his mother and father walked down the plank.
But Dan was sailing the ocean alone,
And he felt a tingle in every bone.

He waved to the pier and stood up tall,
And just as he heard his parents call,
"Good-by Dan!"—they began to get small
Until soon he couldn't see them at all.
Then, as the stacks puffed a farewell toot,
Dan opened the cellophaned basket of fruit.

In the morning Dan used his brush and comb
As the ship rolled high on the wide white foam.
He jumped in the pool for a splashing swim
And tried out a sword in the outdoor gym.
While mothers napped and so did maids,
He teased some girls and pulled their braids.
Then in a deck chair he wrote a line,
Saying that things were extremely fine.

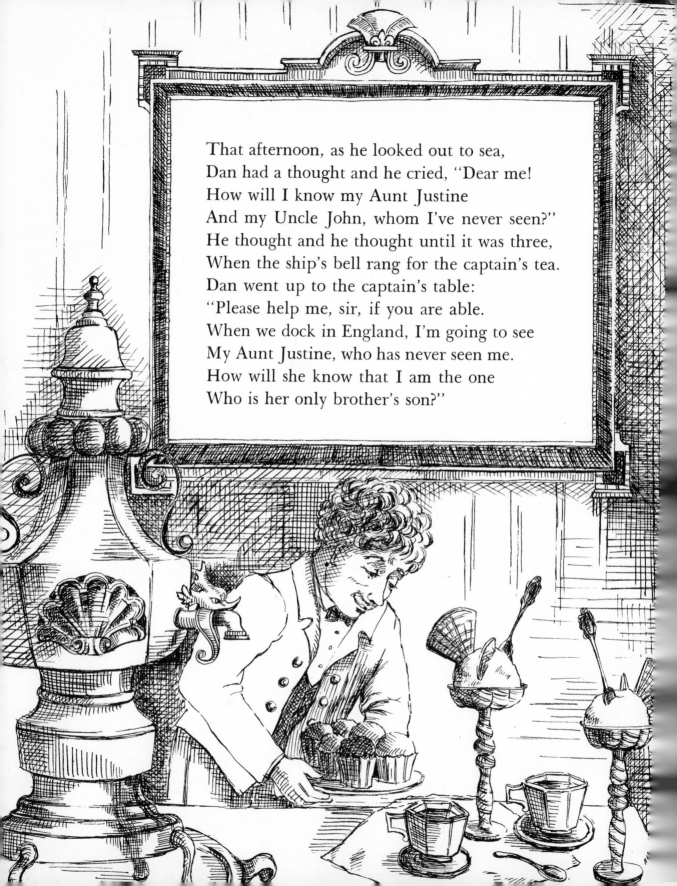

That afternoon, as he looked out to sea,
Dan had a thought and he cried, "Dear me!
How will I know my Aunt Justine
And my Uncle John, whom I've never seen?"
He thought and he thought until it was three,
When the ship's bell rang for the captain's tea.
Dan went up to the captain's table:
"Please help me, sir, if you are able.
When we dock in England, I'm going to see
My Aunt Justine, who has never seen me.
How will she know that I am the one
Who is her only brother's son?"

"Why," said the captain, "that's as easy
As sailing ten knots on a day that's breezy.

"When we arrive and the ship's being towed,
I'll have your name tooted in steamer's Morse code.
And if you like," he winked his eye,
"I'll have some flares thrown in the sky.

"That way, my boy, you need never fear,
Your aunt will know you are on the pier."
"Thank you!" cried Dan, who then, with glee,
Ate four chocolate muffins without any tea.

On the shadowy ship the deck was white.
It was nine o'clock the following night,
And Dan, who should have been in bed,
Was thinking of what the captain said.
"Dear me," thought Dan as the ship's light glowed,
"What if Auntie doesn't know Morse code?"
And he sighed as he looked at the great green sea,
"Oh, how will she ever know I am me?"

Then Dan heard music from the big ship's hall,
And he knew it played for a masquerade ball.
He ran up the stairs and into the rooms
Where people were dancing in masks and plumes.

The bandmaster had a white hat on,
And held in his hand a blue baton.
"Please sir," Dan called, and he looked so forlorn,
The bandmaster hushed the round French horn.
"Please, sir," said Dan, "when we come into port,
Could you blow on the horn a long loud snort;
And then could you say, 'DANNY IS HERE,'
So my aunt will know I'm on the pier?"
"Of course," said the man who led the band,
"I'll take the matter right in hand,
And as we arrive, it will give me great joy
To play for your aunt the tune *Danny Boy*."

Then up spoke a lady who was dressed in a gown
Covered with daisies and wearing a crown:
"Oh, please let us help; it could be a game!
We'll all stand on deck and call out your name;
Your aunt will see us, and to make sure of that,
We will each of us wear our masquerade hat."

"Why, thank you," said Dan, and he caught ten balloons,
While the orchestra played some marvelous tunes.

The day after next, they were due to land,
For the captain spied a strip of sand,
And Danny once more began to fear
He would miss his aunt at Southampton pier.
At breakfast he seemed as pale as a ghost,
And all he could eat was buttered toast.

Then out of the galley marched the cook,
Who stood over Dan with a kindly look.
"I say! Won't you eat just a *little* sardine?"
But all Dan could think of was Aunt Justine.
And he looked through the porthole with tears in his eyes
As the cook tried to tempt him with strawberry pies.

"Let me think," cried the cook. "Ah! I have a plan:
I'll strike up a noise with a spoon and a pan,
And I'll wave to your Aunt from the deck up top,
'Til you run down to meet her when the engines stop."
"Oh, thank you," said Dan, and he gave a great sigh
As he drank some milk with his strawberry pie.

When the ship sailed to port, Danny stood on the stairs,
While the captain sent up twenty-four flares.
As they landed, the passengers all gave a cheer,
And they called to the dock, *"DANNY IS HERE!"*
And the bandmaster played a stirring tune
As the ship's cook beat on a pan with a spoon.

Then everyone thought the ship would explode
As D-A-N came through the smokestacks in code.
There was even a cry from the galley cats
As all of the travelers threw up their hats.

And oh, it was the happiest day,
When Dan ran down the long gangway
And was hugged by a lady he had never seen.
"Why, you must be my Aunt Justine!"
"And you must be Daniel Robert Dufore,
Though I haven't ever seen you before."
"How did you know that I am me?
Did the passengers tell you, or the flares," asked he.
"Did you hear my name in the bandmaster's tune?
Did you see the cook with a pan and a spoon?

"How did you know that I am me?"
"Oh, I think that's very simple," said she.
"Of all the people I see on the pier,
Why, you look most like your father, my dear."